Nothing But
Trouble

White Wolves Series Consultant: Sue Ellis,
Centre for Literacy in Primary Education

This book can be used in the White Wolves Guided Reading
programme with more experienced readers at Year 4 level

First published 2006 by
A & C Black Publishers Ltd
38 Soho Square, London, W1D 3HB

www.acblack.com

ISBN 0-7136-7679-5
ISBN 978-0-7136-7679-2

A CIP catalogue for this book is available from the British Library.

A & C Black uses paper produced with elemental chlorine-free
pulp, harvested from managed sustained forests.

Printed and bound in Great Britain by Bookmarque Ltd, Croydon

Nothing But Trouble

Alan MacDonald

illustrated by Pam Smy

A & C Black • London

Contents

Chapter One

I remember the day I first saw them. I didn't know Jago then but perhaps he was there somewhere, watching us.

We were out on our bikes, Sean and I, when we came upon the caravans by the river. Smoke was curling from a fire. Outside the caravans, people were sitting talking. A few little kids were chasing a barking dog.

"Who are they?" I asked.

"Gypsies," replied Sean.
"Better keep away. My dad says
they're trouble. Don't let them
see your bike or they'll be after it.
They'll steal anything, gypsies.
That's what my dad reckons."

I looked at the people outside
the caravans. They didn't look like
robbers.

"Come on," said Sean. "Let's go back. There's a bad smell around here."

I told Mum about the gypsies. She called them 'travellers' because they move from place to place, never staying long.

"Some people don't like them because of the mess they leave," she said. "Litter and all sorts."

The following Monday, a new boy turned up at our school. Our teacher, Miss Nichols, brought him into the class. He was small and bony with dark, solemn eyes under a tangle of hair.

"This is Jago," said Miss Nichols. "I hope you'll all help him settle in."

Jago scratched his arm. He stared back at us as if we were animals in a zoo.

"Who'd like to be Jago's buddy then? Any volunteers?" asked Miss Nichols.

No one raised their hand.

Miss Nichols looked in my direction. "Paul, what about you?"

She could have chosen anyone. Why did it have to be me? Jago didn't look as if he wanted a buddy. He didn't look as if he wanted anyone.

Jago sat next to me and propped his chin in his hands. All morning he hardly spoke a word. Even when he needed to borrow my rubber, he didn't say 'please'.

I didn't like him much but I was stuck with him. At our school, newcomers are given a buddy on their first day. You're meant to look after them, show them where to go – stuff like that.

It's a good idea but it was just my luck to get someone like Jago.

At lunch time, he trailed after Sean and me, his hands stuffed in his pockets.

"Where do you live?" Sean asked him.

Jago shrugged.

Sean rolled his eyes. "You must live somewhere. What's the name of the road?"

"Isn't a road. It's by the river," replied Jago.

Sean stared at him. "You mean the caravans? You're joking! You're not one of them gypsies?"

Jago lifted his chin and I saw his fists clench. "We're not gypsies," he said.

Luckily Sunil interrupted us. "Are you lot playing or not?" he asked, bouncing his football.

"Any good at football?" I asked Jago.

He gave another shrug, which could have meant anything. He did a lot of shrugging.

Sean muttered in my ear. "We don't want him playing. I bet he doesn't even know the rules."

He spoke softly but Jago must have heard. He turned on Sean.

"What did you say?" he demanded.

"I wasn't talking to you," said Sean. He was bigger than the new boy, but there was something determined about Jago. He didn't look like he'd run from a fight.

"Come on, Sean," I said, pulling him away. "Let's kick off. I'll be in goal."

Jago leaned against the wall, watching us play. In a way I felt sorry for him. He didn't know anyone at our school and I was supposed to be looking out for him. But I couldn't stick with him the whole time. If he didn't want to join in, that was his problem.

Chapter Two

The next day was just as hard
work as the first. It wasn't that
Jago was mean or spiteful to
anyone. He just didn't say much.
Even at lunch he just bent over his
plate and shovelled the food into
his mouth without a word. That
day it was stir-fry chicken and
rice, which is one my favourites.

Half-way through the meal,
I noticed Jago do something odd.

He had hardly touched his chicken, leaving it on one side of the plate. But when he thought no one was looking, he slipped it into a plastic bag. The bag went into his pocket. Glancing up, he caught me staring at him.

"What's that for?" I asked.

"Nothing. I'm keeping it for later."

"You're not allowed food in class."

"So? You're not going to tell on me, are you?"

He went on with eating his rice.

It seemed a funny thing to do – to save scraps of chicken. I kept a close eye on him all afternoon, but he never did eat it. The meat stayed in his pocket the whole time. It was still there when the bell went for the end of school.

I kept wondering what he planned to do with it. Maybe he had brothers or sisters who didn't get enough to eat? There was only one way to find out – I decided to follow him after school. I had an idea he had some reason for keeping the chicken that he didn't want to tell me.

At first I thought he was heading for the river but then he turned off down Stony Street and into Denman Road. I followed at a distance, hiding behind trees and lampposts so that he wouldn't see me. But when I turned the next corner, he was waiting for me. I nearly walked straight into him.

"What are you doing?" he asked, frowning.

"Nothing. Just going home. I live around here."

"Think I'm stupid?" he said. "You've been following me since school."

There wasn't much point in denying it and I didn't want him to get angry. I'd already seen he had a bit of a temper. It seemed safer to tell the truth.

"It's the chicken," I said. "I just want to know what you're going to do with it."

The frown disappeared and Jago burst out laughing. It was the first time I'd even seen him smile.

"All right," he said. "Come on, I'll show you. But it's a secret, OK? Just you and me. You've got to promise."

I promised. By now I was dying of curiosity. What kind of secret could involve a bag of old chicken? Where was he going?

Jago led me along Churchill Street to a house with broken windows and nettles growing in the front. He sauntered down the path as if he owned the place.

I hung back. "Wait!" I said.
"I thought you lived by the river.
Is this your house?"

"No. What's it matter?"

"But you can't just walk in!"

He pointed to a sign by the
front wall that I hadn't noticed.
It said: FOR SALE.

"Empty," he said. "No one lives
here. Come on, if you're coming,
but don't make any noise."

The back garden had a broken
fence and an old, wooden shed.
It was overgrown with weeds.
At the bottom, a thick jungle
of bushes had grown up.

Jago took out the chicken and placed the pieces carefully on the ground. He put a finger to his lips and stepped back.

The two of us crouched behind the shed, hiding.

"What are we waiting for?" I whispered.

"You'll see. Just keep quiet and watch."

Chapter Three

We waited for what seemed ages.
All the time I was worried
someone might come along and
catch us. It felt wrong hiding in
someone else's garden but I didn't
want Jago to think I was scared.
I glanced at him. His eyes were
fixed on the bushes.

Eventually, I heard a rustle of
leaves. The creature came padding
out into the open: a fox, lean and

watchful, eyes black as coal. It
looked around and sniffed the
meat on the ground. A few seconds
later, a second fox appeared, this
one a cub and painfully thin.
We watched as they began to eat
hungrily.

"They've got a den in there,"
Jago whispered. "I followed them
one day. That's the mother; a
vixen she's called."

"I thought foxes live in the woods," I said.

"Not all of them. You get them in towns. They eat mice or birds, steal scraps from dustbins."

We watched in silence while the foxes ate the remains of Jago's lunch. I'd never seen a real fox before – not close up. Their fur wasn't exactly red, it was a sandy, reddish-brown.

The vixen kept glancing around to see if anything was coming. Eventually they finished all the chicken. Then they slunk back into the bushes and were gone.

I realised I'd forgotten the time. Mum would be wondering where I was. "Shall we come back tomorrow?" I asked.

"All right," said Jago. "But remember, you're not to tell anyone else. Especially that big-mouth, Sean."

"OK," I said. I felt pleased that Jago had chosen me to share his secret. He could have kept it to himself but he hadn't.

We parted at the gate. I watched Jago hop onto the front wall of a house and walk along it as if balancing on a tightrope.

He jumped down and gave me a wave. "See you tomorrow!"

Over the next weeks we visited the foxes maybe a dozen times. At lunch I always tried to save some of my meat and so did Jago.

When no one was looking he would slip it into the plastic bag under the table. After school we would meet on the corner of Denman Road and make our way to the fox house. We didn't want anyone following us.

Sometimes the foxes weren't there – or maybe they were asleep in their den. Other times they came out after only a few minutes.

One day, Jago didn't hide behind the shed. He put the meat on the ground and sat down beside it, in the middle of the garden. For a long time the foxes

wouldn't come out but we could
see a pair of black eyes watching
us from the bushes.

At last the vixen crept into view.
She picked up the meat in her
teeth and vanished into her den.

"See?" said Jago, delighted.
"She's learning to trust us."

The next time he tried
something more daring. He placed
a piece of chicken on the palm
of his hand and held it out. He

wanted to see if they would take it from him. I held my breath, trying not to fidget. I knew any sudden movement would frighten them and they wouldn't come out at all.

"They're not pets," Jago had warned me. "They're wild."

For ages we sat there, keeping still as the grave. At last the vixen nosed out of the bushes but she wasn't prepared to come too close. In the end it was the little cub that made a move. It darted out of the brambles and snatched the chicken out of Jago's hand. Then it turned tail and disappeared with the mother on its heels.

Jago turned to me with a look of pure wonder on his face. "Did you see that?" he asked. "Took it right out of my hand! Right out of my hand!"

Everyone at school thought Jago was sullen and moody because he didn't say much. But the Jago I knew was different. With me he laughed and talked and fooled around. Sometimes we pretended everyone we met on the street was a spy and we had to get to the fox house without being seen. The more I got to know Jago, the more I began to like him.

There was just one problem – Sean. He didn't like Jago one bit and was always trying to put him down with snide little remarks. It was as if he wanted to needle him, push him into losing his temper.

"Why do you put up with him?" Sean asked me once.

"I've got to," I said. "I'm meant to be his buddy."

"That was only when he started. You don't have to keep it up for ever!"

"He's OK," I said. "You just have to get to know him."

Sean screwed up his nose. "No, thanks. He gives me the creeps, following you round like a dog all the time. You should be careful, Paul. Remember what I told you?"

I shook my head. "I told you, he's not a thief."

Sean laughed dryly. "He's a gypsy. That's the same thing, isn't it?"

I could tell Jago got sick of the needling, and sometimes he answered back. Meanwhile I was stuck in the middle. They were both my friends but they hated the sight of each other. Looking back, I should have seen the trouble coming.

Chapter Four

It was a Friday when things
finally came to a head. Jago
had been at our school for almost
a month. The
following week
our class was
going on
a trip to
Sea Life.

Sean and I had been excited about it ever since the visit was announced.

At the start of break I was looking for Sean. Finally I tracked him down to the cloakroom, where I found him rummaging in his school bag.

"Come on!" I said. "Aren't you coming out?"

He shook his head. "In a minute. I can't find my money for the trip."

Sean emptied his bag out onto the floor, spilling books and papers. "It's not here!" he said, hopelessly.

"Maybe you left it at home?" I suggested.

"I didn't! My mum gave me three pounds this morning. I remember putting it in the pocket of my bag so it would be safe."

"Then it must be there," I said.

"It's not! I've checked a million times." He looked at me. "No, somebody took it and I bet I know who."

If Jago hadn't appeared at that moment, Sean might have calmed down. It was just unlucky that he happened to pass by.

Sean called him back. "Hey, Jago! Come here!"

"What?" said Jago, stopping.

"Where is it?" demanded Sean.

Jago raised his eyebrows and glanced at me. "Where's what?"

"Think it's a joke, do you?" said Sean. "Think it's funny?"

"Dunno what you're talking about."

"Stealing my money. There was three pounds in my bag this morning."

"Come on, Sean," I pleaded. "It's nothing to do with him. Let him go."

I could see where this was heading. But Sean wouldn't let it drop.

"I can see it in your face," he said. "You took it!"

Jago shook his head. "You're bonkers. I haven't been anywhere near your stupid bag."

"Liar! I saw you hanging round the cloakroom this morning."

"I was looking for Paul," said Jago.

"Yeah right," said Sean. "You were waiting till everyone had gone. You're a thief like all your lot."

Jago's face turned red. He clenched his fists. I had seen that wild look in his eyes before.

"Show us your pockets," ordered Sean.

"Make me," said Jago.

The next minute they were at each other. Sean was big for his age and shoved Jago hard back against the wall.

But Jago fought like a wildcat and soon he'd wrestled Sean to the floor. They rolled over and over, panting and grunting. Sean had his hand over Jago's mouth. Some of our year had gathered round to watch the fight. Then I saw Miss Nichols walking swiftly in our direction. She must have heard the commotion.

Jago was sitting on top of Sean, pinning him to the floor.

"Pack it in!" I warned. "There's a teacher coming!"

But it was too late. The crowd parted and Miss Nichols caught hold of Jago's arm.

"OFF! Get off him at once, Jago!" she shouted. "What *do* you think you're doing?"

The two of them got to their feet and stood glaring at each other, red in the face and breathing hard. Sean had lost a button from his shirt.

Miss Nichols turned on the bystanders. "Outside! All of you! NOW!" She clapped her hands and they scattered like a flock of sparrows. I hung around, not sure whether to stay or go.

"Now then, what's this all about?" Miss Nichols demanded.

"Ask him," said Sean, pointing at Jago.

"Well, Jago?"

Jago just wiped his mouth.

"He stole my trip money," said Sean. "It was in my bag."

"Is this true?" asked Miss Nichols.

Jago's eyes blazed. "No."

"Then why were you fighting?"

"He started it," said Sean. "He jumped on me."

"Liar!" said Jago. "He called me a thief!"

"That's enough!" thundered Miss Nichols. "You will both come now to the Head's office and explain yourselves." She turned to me. "Paul, you were here. Did you see what happened?"

I hesitated. I'd been hoping Miss Nichols wouldn't ask me.

Sean turned to me. "It was him that started it, wasn't it, Paul? Tell her."

Miss Nichols waited for me to answer. I could feel my face had gone red. Sean wanted me to back him up, to put the blame on Jago. But it wasn't really true, if anyone had started the fight it was Sean. All the same, I didn't want to get him into trouble.

"Well?" said Miss Nichols.

"I didn't really see," I said. "All of a sudden they just started fighting."

"Hmm," said Miss Nichols with a suspicious look at me. "Right you two, follow me."

Miss Nichols led them up the stairs to the Head's office. As Sean passed, he stared at me coldly. I could tell he felt I'd let him down. Best friends are supposed to stick together, aren't they?

Chapter Five

After school I waited at the corner
of Denman Road as usual. I didn't
know whether Jago
would come after
all the trouble,
but he did.

"What happened?" I asked. There hadn't been a chance to speak since the fight as Sean had always been prowling nearby.

He shrugged. "Nothing much. The Head gave us a lecture. Said I wouldn't be going on the trip. I'm not fussed, I wasn't going anyway."

"Why not?" I asked.

He didn't answer, but fished in his pocket. "I've saved some meat," he said. "Let's go and see the foxes."

We hadn't been back to the house for two days but in that time

something had changed. The FOR
SALE sign was missing from the
front garden and a plume of grey
smoke rose from the back.

"There's somebody there,"
I said to Jago.

We crept down the drive, Jago
going first and me following
behind. Peering round the corner
of the wall, we saw two workmen.

A smoky bonfire was burning in the middle of the garden. One man was cutting down the nettles and bushes with a buzzing machine. The other used a fork to load the fallen brambles onto the fire. The jungle of bushes had almost disappeared. I stared at the scene in dismay.

"Wait!" shouted Jago, going right up to the workmen.

"Stone me! Where did you two spring from?" said one of them, looking up in surprise. He had a round, red face flecked with stubble.

"You can't do that!" said Jago.

"Who says we can't? The owner wants this lot cleared."

"You don't understand," I said. "There are foxes living here. A mother and a cub."

The red-faced workman shrugged his shoulders. "Not seen any foxes, have we, Ray? But if we do I'll be glad to kill the little devils. Dirty vermin they are."

"You're a pig!" said Jago, unexpectedly. "A fat pig! Leave them alone!" The workman was twice his size, but he aimed a punch at him.

"You clear off, son, before I clout you," growled the workman. "This is private property!" He raised his fork in the air and started to advance towards us.

We turned and ran. We ran down Churchill Road and ducked into the alley. When we were sure they weren't chasing us, we slowed to a walk.

"What are we going to do now?" I asked.

"Dunno," said Jago. "Just hope the foxes got away. The noise would have frightened them off."

"But what if they didn't get away? Those men are burning the bushes!"

Jago kicked a stone along the alley. "What can we do? Nobody's going to listen to us, are they?"

He was right. The garden didn't belong to us and the foxes had no more right to be there than we did. We'd reached the allotments, where a muddy path ran down to the river.

"Come on," Jago said. "I want to show you something."

When we reached the travellers' camp, he stopped. The fire had been stamped out. The travellers were moving around, packing up their things.

"You're going?" I said in dismay. "Why?"

"Got to," said Jago. "Council says we've got to move on."

"Where to?"

"Dunno. Somewhere north. I was going to tell you this morning. That's why I was looking for you at school."

It didn't seem fair. First I had lost the foxes and now Jago was leaving. It was only now I realised how much I was going to miss him.

"So I won't see you again?"
I said.

"Not for a while. We might
come back some day. Anyway…"
He held out his hand awkwardly.
"I wanted to say … you know,
thanks."

"For what?" I asked.

"Being my 'buddy' at school!" He laughed. "I know it wasn't your idea."

We shook hands and smiled, not sure what else to say. A woman's voice called his name.

"Better go," said Jago and ran off towards the caravans.

I stood for a while, watching the travellers packing up. Jago waved to me from the steps of his caravan before the door closed. Then I turned to go, following the riverside path back towards my house.

Turning the bend, the path led through a small wood. It was then I thought I saw them in the grass ahead of me: two foxes, a vixen and her skinny little cub, standing in a bright patch of sunlight.

When I looked again they were gone. Maybe I just imagined it, I don't know, but I like to think they came back to say goodbye. That's how foxes live, I thought, always moving on, never welcome.

I hope they found a new home.

About the Author

Alan MacDonald was born in Watford and now lives near the River Trent in Nottingham. At school his ambition was to become a footballer, but then he won a pen in a writing competition and his fate was sealed.

He spent several years in a travelling theatre company before turning full time to writing in 1990. Since then he has published more than 50 books for children, ranging from picture books to novels and non fiction.

WHITE WOLVES